GW00455967

FOREWORD

Welcome, dear readers, to the captivating world of words, where creativity reigns supreme and excuses take center stage. Within the pages of this extraordinary volume of "The Wordsmith's Arsenal," we embark on a delightful journey that explores the delicate balance between legitimate excuses and lighthearted banter when it comes to forgetting someone's birthday.

Birthdays, those cherished moments that commemorate the passage of time, hold great significance in our lives. They provide an opportunity for celebration, reflection, and showing appreciation for the special individuals who grace our existence. Yet, despite our best intentions, the hustle and bustle of life can sometimes cause us to momentarily forget these important dates.

In the first part of this volume, we delve into a collection of legitimate excuses, meticulously crafted to offer sincere explanations for those instances when forgetfulness gets the better of us. These excuses are grounded in reality, acknowledging genuine circumstances and experiences that may lead to a temporary lapse in memory. They provide a way to express remorse, understanding, and a genuine desire to make amends for the unintentional oversight.

However, as we turn the pages and venture into the second part of this volume, we enter the realm of banter and playfulness. Here, we explore a delightful array of excuses that, while not entirely plausible, ignite laughter, camaraderie, and a sense of whimsy.

These excuses dance at the intersection of imagination and humor, where creativity takes flight and mundane forgetfulness transforms into comedic tales that tickle the funny bone.

However, dear readers, it is essential to remember the delicate balance between genuine remorse and lighthearted banter. While the second part of this volume explores excuses that inspire laughter, it is crucial to gauge the recipient's sense of humor and the nature of your relationship. Always accompany these playful explanations with a heartfelt apology, ensuring that the underlying care and consideration shine through the laughter.

So, dear readers, embark on this enchanting journey through "The Wordsmith's Arsenal: Excuses for Forgetting Someone's Birthday." Discover the art of crafting legitimate explanations and embrace the joy that comes with sprinkling a touch of banter into our relationships. May these pages serve as a reminder that, even in forgetfulness, we can connect, uplift, and create lasting memories through the power of words and laughter.

Happy reading, and may your excuses be as genuine as they are whimsical, forging deeper bonds and infusing life's forgetful moments with warmth and mirth!

EXCUSES

By keeping these points in mind, you can approach the excuse-giving process with sincerity, empathy, and a genuine desire to rebuild the connection that may have been momentarily disrupted by forgetfulness:

1. Timing: Offer your excuse as soon as possible after realizing your mistake. Delaying the apology may diminish its impact and make it appear insincere.

2. Honesty: While it's important to inject humor and creativity into your excuse, ensure that it remains grounded in truth. Exaggerations or outright lies can undermine the sincerity of your apology.

3. Empathy: Put yourself in the other person's shoes and consider how they might feel about your forgetfulness. Show empathy and understanding for any disappointment or hurt they may have experienced.

4. Take responsibility: Accept full responsibility for forgetting their birthday. Avoid shifting blame or making excuses that come across as dismissive or insincere.

5. Apologize sincerely: Offer a heartfelt apology that acknowledges the impact of your forgetfulness and demonstrates genuine remorse. Let the person know that you understand the significance of their birthday and that you deeply regret your oversight.

6. Be specific: Provide a clear and concise explanation for why you forgot their birthday. This helps to show that it was an honest mistake rather than a lack of consideration.

7. Avoid trivializing: While humor can help lighten the mood, be careful not to trivialize the importance of their birthday or downplay their feelings. Strike a balance between humor and genuine remorse.

8. Make amends: Offer to make it up to them by planning a belated celebration, giving a thoughtful gift, or spending quality time together. Actions speak louder than words, and showing your commitment to making it right is crucial.

9. Learn and improve: Express a genuine desire to improve your memory and organizational skills. Let the person know that you're taking steps to prevent such oversights in the future, reinforcing your commitment to the relationship.

10. Listen and communicate: Give the person an opportunity to express their feelings and concerns. Listen attentively, validate their emotions, and communicate openly to ensure that you understand their perspective.

With that in mind here are 15 of the best excuses

Calendar Malfunction: Apologize for the oversight and explain that there was a technical issue with your digital calendar, causing it to skip or not remind you of important dates.

Busy Schedule: Apologize for being caught up in a hectic period of work or personal commitments, causing you to overlook the birthday celebration.

Personal Crisis: Express that you were dealing with an unexpected personal crisis that consumed your attention and made you unintentionally forget their birthday.

Family Emergency: Inform them that a family emergency arose, demanding your immediate attention and distracting you from remembering the important occasion.

Travel Disruption: Explain that you were traveling and faced unexpected disruptions or complications that threw off your schedule and made it difficult to keep track of dates.

Health Issues: Apologize for having been unwell or dealing with health-related concerns, which resulted in your unintentional oversight of their birthday.

Memory Lapse: Admit to having a temporary lapse in memory due to stress or exhaustion, causing you to forget their special day.

Social Media Glitch: Mention that you rely on social media for birthday reminders, but due to a technical glitch, you missed their notification or birthday announcement.

Misplaced Invitation: Apologize for losing or misplacing the invitation to their birthday celebration, which led to your unintentional absence.

Busy Social Calendar: Explain that you had a string of other birthdays and social events around the same time, which caused you to mix up the dates and inadvertently overlook theirs.

Personal Milestone: Share that you had a personal milestone or important event in your own life that coincided with their birthday, momentarily diverting your attention.

Work Overload: Apologize for being buried under a heavy workload or pressing deadlines at work, making it difficult to remember important dates, including their birthday.

Change in Routine: Mention that a recent change in your daily routine disrupted your usual pattern of checking and remembering birthdays, resulting in the oversight.

Time Zone Confusion: If you're in different time zones, explain that the time difference caused confusion and made it challenging to remember their birthday accurately.

Post Office Delay: If you planned to send them a physical gift or card, blame a postal delay or mix-up for the late arrival, which led to the belated acknowledgment of their special day.

HUMOUR

When using humour as an excuse for forgetting someone's birthday, here are some tips and things to keep in mind:

1. Know your audience: Consider the person's sense of humor and their receptiveness to playful banter. Tailor your excuse to their personality to ensure it will be well-received.

2. Light-hearted tone: Maintain a light-hearted and playful tone throughout your excuse. The goal is to evoke laughter and create a positive atmosphere.

3. Balance sincerity and humor: While humor is essential, ensure that your excuse still conveys genuine remorse for forgetting their birthday. Strike a balance between sincerity and comedic elements.

4. Avoid offensive humor: Stay away from jokes or remarks that may be offensive, insensitive, or hurtful. Your excuse should bring joy and laughter, not cause discomfort or distress.

5. Be creative and imaginative: Infuse your excuse with creativity and imagination. Think outside the box to come up with amusing scenarios or unexpected events that explain your forgetfulness.

6. Keep it believable: While creativity is encouraged, ensure that your excuse remains believable. Exaggerations or far-fetched stories may come across as insincere or implausible.

7. Self-deprecating humor: Incorporate self-deprecating humor to show that you can laugh at yourself. It helps to lighten the mood and avoid any perception of defensiveness.

8. Emphasize the positive: Focus on the positive aspects of your relationship and the value you place on the person whose birthday you forgot. Use humor to highlight the love, friendship, or special moments you share.

9. Use funny anecdotes or metaphors: Share amusing anecdotes or create metaphors that paint a picture of your forgetfulness. These storytelling elements can add an extra layer of humor to your excuse.

10. Follow up with a genuine apology: While humor is effective in diffusing tension, always follow it up with a sincere apology. Show that you genuinely regret forgetting their birthday and that you understand the significance of the occasion.

Remember, humor is subjective, and what may be funny to one person may not be to another. Consider your relationship with the person and their individual preferences. When in doubt, err on the side of caution and choose humor that is light-hearted, inclusive, and uplifting.

Here are some humours excuses to help you in the heat of the moment:

> "Your birthday coincided with the national day of procrastination. I'll make it up to you... eventually."

"I didn't forget your birthday; I was just waiting for it to become a national holiday so we could all have the day off."

"I was so mesmerized by your eternal youth that I forgot to acknowledge the passing of time. Happy belated birthday, forever young!"

"My dog ate my birthday reminder. Note to self: Get a dog that doesn't have a sweet tooth for calendars."

"I didn't forget your birthday; I just didn't want you to feel too special, so I celebrated your 'unbirthday' instead."

"I didn't forget your birthday; I was just trying to be fashionably late. Fashionistas never arrive on time!"

"I didn't forget your birthday; I was just trying to create suspense, like they do in suspenseful movies. Happy belated birthday, the sequel!"

"I wanted to give you the full experience of being a celebrity. You know, celebrating your birthday a little later than everyone else. You're welcome!"

"I was planning a surprise party for you, but it got so massive and extravagant that it took me a little longer to organize.

Get ready for the most epic belated birthday bash!"

"I didn't forget your birthday; I was just giving you an opportunity to appreciate how much you mean to me every single day, not just on your actual birthday."

"You see, I have a talent for making birthdays unforgettable, even if it means celebrating them a little later. It's all part of my master plan!"

"I didn't forget your birthday; I just wanted to keep you in suspense, wondering when the fabulous celebration would take place. Surprise!"

"I was so mesmerized by your awesomeness that I lost track of time and completely forgot it was your birthday. My bad!"

"I was waiting for the perfect alignment of the stars and the universe to celebrate your birthday. It took a bit longer than expected, but it'll be worth the wait!"

"I didn't forget your birthday; I just wanted to see if you'd make it into the Guinness World Records for having the longest birthday celebration ever. You're on track!"

"Your birthday was on my to-do list, but it accidentally fell into a time vortex. I'm working on retrieving it, I promise!"

"I was so busy thinking of an incredible birthday surprise that I got lost in my own imagination and forgot to actually plan anything. Next year, prepare for the most mind-blowing celebration!"

"I didn't forget your birthday; I was just celebrating it on a different dimensional plane. It's a little-known secret that time works differently there."

"You know, age is just a number, and I was giving you a break from the whole aging process. Consider it a gift!"

"I was so determined to find the perfect gift that I got lost in a maze of online shopping and completely lost track of time. Expect something truly amazing!"

"I didn't forget your birthday; I just thought it would be more memorable if we celebrated it on a non-traditional day. Who needs conventionality?"

"I was so inspired by your unique personality that I decided to celebrate your birthday on a different calendar altogether. Embrace the eccentricity!"

"I didn't forget your birthday; I was just following the 'fashionably late' trend. You know, being fashion-forward and all."

"I didn't forget your birthday; I was simply stretching out the celebration to make it last longer. Now it's a birthday extravaganza!"

"I didn't forget your birthday; I just wanted to see if you'd be cool enough to celebrate it on the same day as a holiday. Double the fun!"

"I didn't forget your birthday; I was just participating in a memory championship, and ironically, your birthday slipped my mind."

"I was so captivated by your magnetic personality that I got temporarily distracted and accidentally overlooked your birthday. But don't worry, you're unforgettable!"

"I didn't forget your birthday; I was just giving you an opportunity to feel extra special by having two days of celebration. You're worth it!"

"I was trying to set a new world record for the latest birthday wish ever. It's all about pushing boundaries and making history!"

"I didn't forget your birthday; I was just waiting for the perfect moment to surprise you. It turns out, I'm really good at keeping secrets!"

"I didn't forget your birthday; I was just giving you a break from the annual reminder that time is passing by. Think of it as a gift of eternal youth!"

"Your birthday was so amazing that it temporarily overloaded my memory circuits. But now that I've rebooted, belated happy birthday!"

"I didn't forget your birthday; I was just participating in an experiment to see how people react when their special day is delayed. Consider it a social study!"

"I was so mesmerized by your incredible existence that I lost track of time and completely missed your birthday. You have that effect on me!"

"I didn't forget your birthday; I just wanted to give you a taste of what life would be like without birthdays. Spoiler alert: it's not as fun!"

"I was trapped in a time loop, and unfortunately, your birthday was one of the days that got caught in the loop. But hey, now we have an extra day to celebrate!"

"I didn't forget your birthday; I was simply waiting for the perfect alignment of the stars, planets, and unicorns. Now it's time for a cosmic celebration!"

"I was temporarily banished to a land where birthdays don't exist, and I mistakenly lingered there longer than I intended. But I'm back now, ready to celebrate!"

"I didn't forget your birthday; I was just waiting for the most epic birthday party theme to come to me in a dream. It took a bit longer than expected, but get ready for an unforgettable celebration!"

"I didn't forget your birthday; I was just giving you an opportunity to practice patience and forgiveness. Consider it a character-building exercise!"

"Your birthday was actually too memorable that I needed some extra time to recover from all the festivities. Happy belated birthday, and sorry for the delayed response!"

"I didn't forget your birthday; I was just on a top-secret mission to save the world from boredom. Now that it's accomplished, let's celebrate!"

"I was abducted by aliens on your birthday, and they accidentally wiped my memory of the event. But I managed to escape and remember now. Happy belated birthday, Earthling!"

"I didn't forget your birthday; I was just giving you a chance to experience the anticipation and excitement of waiting for your special day. It's all about building the suspense!"

"Your birthday is so special that it requires a longer celebration period. That's why I'm fashionably late with my wishes. Enjoy the extended festivities!"

"I didn't forget your birthday; I was just running on 'birthday time,' which means I celebrate it whenever I want. And right now, it's the perfect time to wish you a happy belated birthday!"

"I was too busy solving complex mathematical equations that prove how age is just an illusion. Don't worry; I'll spare you the details. Belated happy birthday!"

"I didn't forget your birthday; I was just trapped in a parallel universe where time works differently. Now that I'm back, let's party like it's your birthday!"

"Your birthday was so extraordinary that I needed extra time to come up with an equally extraordinary wish. So here it is: Happy belated birthday to the most extraordinary person!"

"Oh, come on! I didn't forget your birthday, I just wanted to see if you'd notice. Surprise!"

"Of course, I didn't forget your birthday. I was just testing your reaction time to see how quickly you'd realize it."

"Well, I was actually planning to celebrate your birthday for the entire month, but I got carried away and lost track of time. Happy belated birthday!"

"I didn't forget your birthday; I was just trying to extend the celebration. Who wants just one day when we can have a birth-week or even a birth-month?"

"You know what they say, the best gifts are the ones that arrive fashionably late. So, happy fashionable belated birthday!"

"I'm sorry I forgot your birthday, but in my defense, I've been celebrating my 'Forgetful Friend of the Year' award. It's a big honor, you know!"

"I purposely forgot your birthday so that you can have a 'birth-month' and enjoy the spotlight for a little longer. You're welcome!"

"I didn't forget your birthday; I was just trying to create suspense and build up the excitement. It's all part of the grand birthday masterplan."

"You know, age is just a number, and I wanted to spare you from the trauma of adding another one. You're welcome for the temporary age freeze!"

"Oh, I'm sorry, I didn't realize your birthday was a national holiday that I should have marked on my calendar. My bad!"

"I wanted to see if you were one of those people who actually cared about their birthday. Congrats, you passed the test!"

"I didn't forget your birthday; I just wanted to give you a taste of what life would be like without my amazing birthday wishes. You're welcome!"

"I intentionally forgot your birthday to keep you humble. Can't have you getting too big-headed about turning another year older!"

"I figured you're one of those people who doesn't want any attention on their birthday, so I graciously spared you the hassle."

"I was planning a surprise party for you, but then I realized you're too old for surprises. So, I saved us all the effort."

"Oh, did I forget your birthday? My mind must have been too preoccupied with important things, like, um, literally anything else."

"I didn't forget your birthday; I was just busy commemorating the invention of sliced bread. It's a big deal, you know?"

"Your birthday got lost in the Bermuda Triangle of my brain. Strange how that happens, right?"

"I was so mesmerized by the incredible number of candles I'd need for your cake that I got overwhelmed and just gave up."

"I didn't forget your birthday; I was just trying to save money on presents. You should thank me for being frugal!"

"You know, age is just a number, so I thought it wouldn't matter if I forgot to acknowledge yet another number."

"I didn't forget your birthday; I just wanted to give you a break from all the hype and hoopla. You're welcome for the peace and quiet!"

"I was too busy planning my own birthday extravaganza that I temporarily forgot about yours. Sorry, but my party is going to be way better."

"I didn't forget your birthday; I just wanted to give you a challenge to see how long it would take you to remind me."

"Oh, your birthday? I didn't forget. I intentionally didn't mention it to save you from the embarrassment of getting older."

"I didn't forget your birthday; I was just testing your memory to see if you'd remember mine in return. You failed!"

"Your birthday? I didn't forget; I was just too busy being fabulous to acknowledge it properly."

"I was too caught up in the excitement of my own life that I completely overlooked the fact that you have one too. Oops!"

"I didn't forget your birthday; I was just waiting for the perfect opportunity to surprise you with an even better celebration. Be patient!"

EPILOGUE

In the realm of forgetfulness and the art of excuses, we find ourselves at the end of this journey through "The Wordsmith's Arsenal: Excuses for Forgetting Someone's Birthday." It has been a whimsical adventure, filled with laughter, banter, and moments of reflection. As we bid farewell, let us take a moment to reflect on the lessons learned and the connections forged.

Forgetting someone's birthday is a human error that can sometimes lead to hurt feelings and misunderstandings. Yet, within the realm of excuses, we discovered the power of laughter and creativity in navigating these delicate situations. We learned that a well-crafted excuse, whether it be sincere, witty, sarcastic, or sassy, has the potential to mend bonds, ignite joy, and remind us of the resilience of our relationships.

However, let us not forget that excuses are only a means to an end. The true value lies in the sincerity behind them, the heartfelt apologies, and the actions taken to make amends. As we close this chapter, let us carry with us the importance of thoughtfulness, attentiveness, and genuine care for the ones we hold dear.

Remember, birthdays are not merely dates on a calendar, but celebrations of life, love, and the unique individuals who grace our journey. May we take these experiences and apply them to all aspects of our relationships, making every day an opportunity to celebrate and appreciate those around us.

As the curtain falls on "The Wordsmith's Arsenal: Excuses for Forgetting Someone's Birthday," may the memories created and the laughter shared continue to resonate in our hearts. Let us go forth, armed with the power of words, compassion, and an unwavering commitment to treasuring the special moments and the people who make our lives brighter.

Farewell, dear readers, and may your excuses always be accompanied by heartfelt apologies, genuine gestures of kindness, and a celebration of the beautiful connections that enrich our lives.

Printed in Great Britain
by Amazon

29462163R00015